★ American Girl®

forever friends

Jasmine's Big Idea

🐾 By Crystal Velasquez 🐾

SCHOLASTIC INC.

To Bandit, the best dog I ever had.
–C.V.

Published by Scholastic Inc., *Publishers since 1920.* SCHOLASTIC and associated logos are trademarks and/or registered trademarks of Scholastic Inc. The publisher does not have any control over and does not assume any responsibility for author or third-party websites or their content.

This book is a work of fiction. Names, characters, places, and incidents are either the product of the author's imagination or are used fictitiously, and any resemblance to actual persons, living or dead, business establishments, events, or locales is entirely coincidental.

Book design by Baily Crawford

ISBN 978-1-338-11491-1

10 9 8 7 6 5 4 3 2 1   17 18 19 20 21

Printed in the U.S.A.   23

First printing 2017

Table of Contents

Jasmine Arroyo had never seen anything cuter than the litter of six-week-old kittens. Well, her own dog, Cookie—her eighth birthday present—was pretty adorable. But with the kittens, the cuteness factor was multiplied by five. They stared up at her with curious eyes, mewing loudly.

"They're a noisy bunch, aren't they?" her mom, Dr. Lydia Arroyo, said as she swept into the room at the animal shelter where the younger cats and kittens stayed.

Jasmine kneeled to get a closer look. The kittens had come in three days ago, along with their mother. The director of the shelter, Rosa Wallace, had settled them into a cozy cage on the second shelf against the wall. But when Jasmine came to meet them, Mrs. Wallace moved the litter into a large cardboard box on the floor, its bottom lined with newspaper and soft old towels.

Jasmine had instantly fallen in love with all five of them.

"Making a lot of noise is a good sign, right?" she asked her mom.

"It is," Jasmine's mom answered with a

smile. "It means they're getting stronger. Playing with them helps."

Jasmine smiled and reached into the large box. She gently pet the kitten she had named Tiger between his silky brown ears. She noticed that his fur was almost the same color as her own corkscrew curls. Tiger purred, then squirmed to the side and pounced on her hand.

Jasmine's mom was a veterinarian, a doctor who helps animals. Thanks to her mom, Jasmine knew pets needed things like certain kinds of food, plenty of water, and sometimes medicine to stay healthy. But since she had started volunteering at the animal shelter every Saturday, Jasmine had learned that petting and playing with the dogs and cats were just as important. Mrs. Wallace said the animals had to get used to being around humans and other animals before they could be adopted.

"Thanks again for coming in today," Mrs. Wallace said as she carried in a grocery bag of canned cat food. She smiled warmly at Jasmine, straightening her thick glasses. The glasses were the only sign that Mrs. Wallace was close to retirement age. Her dark brown skin was wrinkle free except for the tiny crinkles that appeared around her mouth when she smiled.

"Because of your mom, *their* mom will soon be healthy enough to take care of these little guys again," Mrs. Wallace said as she nodded at the kittens. They had begun burrowing into the folds of the towels. "At least until they're a bit older and we find them forever homes."

When anyone brought in stray or abandoned animals, Mrs. Wallace and her husband took them in, made sure they were healthy, and then found them new, loving families. Jasmine thought it sounded like a hard but wonderful job.

"It's my pleasure," Dr. Arroyo said as she took off her white coat and draped it over her arm. "But it's close to dinnertime. We'd better get going, Jaz."

"Aw, Mom, do we have to go already?" Jasmine protested. "I was going to help walk the dogs and maybe feed the kittens . . ."

"That's sweet of you, Jasmine," said Mrs. Wallace, "but Mr. Wallace will be along soon to walk the dogs, and I think these little ones have plans of their own."

She gestured toward the box. The kittens were huddled together, fast asleep.

Jasmine hated leaving the shelter. If she could, she would come by every chance she got. She hoped to be a veterinarian one day, just like her mom.

"All right," she said, reluctantly getting to her feet. "I'll see you next Saturday. I just wish there was more we could do for them now."

Mrs. Wallace took a step toward Jasmine and Dr. Arroyo, her eyes sparkling. "Well, maybe there's something you could do for all the animals, actually," she said. Then she motioned for Jasmine and her mom to follow her. They trailed Mrs. Wallace out of the cat room, across the shelter lobby, and right through the front door.

Rosa's Refuge Animal Shelter was housed in a cozy one-story brick building with separate areas for cats, puppies, and larger breeds. There were also private rooms where people could play with animals before they adopted them. And the small, fenced-in yard behind the shelter served as a dog run.

Mrs. Wallace pointed to the empty storefront next to the shelter. A large red FOR SALE sign hung in the window.

"I'm sure you've noticed how busy we've been at the shelter lately. We need more space so that we can take in all the animals that are homeless or between homes. Right now, we have to turn quite a few away. My husband and

I would like to buy this store and make it part of our shelter."

Mrs. Wallace sighed. "But we would need to raise a lot more money to buy the store and remodel it to house animals. I'd love to have a community fund-raiser, but I'm so busy at the shelter, I could really use some help organizing it."

Suddenly, Jasmine had an idea. She looked up at her mom eagerly, her eyes shining.

"Mom, we could help with a fund-raiser, couldn't we?" she asked hopefully.

Her mom smiled.

"I don't see why not," she agreed warmly.

"My mom helped the PTA plan the spring fair at my school last year," Jasmine continued excitedly. "We raised a lot of money to buy books for the library."

"That sounds wonderful," Mrs. Wallace replied. "I was thinking of a carnival in the park across the street. My friend has a small petting zoo that he could set up, and we could have a bounce castle and sell some Rosa's Refuge T-shirts. We could even ask local businesses to match the donations we raise. With any luck, we'll have our adopt-a-cat trailer out, and we can get some people to take home a new pet!"

"And we could raffle off prizes!" Jasmine suggested. "We did that at the school fair, and it was so fun. We also had a really cool arts-and-crafts area. Maybe we could do that, too."

"Those are terrific ideas, Jasmine," Mrs. Wallace said. "In fact, how would you like to be my assistant carnival planner? I could really use your ideas and opinions about fun activities for kids."

Jasmine bounced up and down. "Ooh, Mom!" she said excitedly. "Can I do it? Can I? I already have ideas for signs and decorations . . ."

Jasmine got a determined gleam in her eye that her mom instantly recognized. Dr. Arroyo couldn't help but grin at her daughter's enthusiasm.

"I think it's a wonderful idea," Dr. Arroyo said. Mrs. Wallace nodded in agreement. "Now, what do you say we get home for dinner? Your father's making *pastelón*."

Jasmine's mouth watered. She loved her dad's Puerto Rican lasagna.

"Sounds good, Mom," Jasmine replied as they waved good-bye to Mrs. Wallace and headed to their car.

"You're awfully quiet," Dr. Arroyo said as they walked. "You were so excited just a moment ago."

"I was just thinking of something Mrs. Wallace said," Jasmine replied slowly. "What happens to the animals that Rosa's Refuge turns away?"

Her mom grew serious. "If they can't find them homes, they have to put them to sleep," Dr. Arroyo explained gently, putting her arm around her daughter. "It's very sad, *niña.*"

"Oh!" Jasmine said, shocked. No wonder Mrs. Wallace wanted to make the shelter larger. "That's terrible, Mom. Now I realize how important this carnival is. I just *have* to help."

"I know you do, *niña*," her mom replied.

Jasmine was sure they would need more help to make the carnival a success. And she knew just the friends she wanted to ask.

Chapter 2

Doggie Drama

The next day, Jasmine invited her best friends, Keiko Hayashi and Sofia Davis, over to her house.

Since it was warm outside, they decided to play soccer in the backyard. Sofia had joined the neighborhood soccer team the year before, and she loved showing her friends the new moves she had learned.

"This one's called an inside rollover," Sofia said. She gently kicked the ball, then ran her right foot over the top, sending it flying to the left. Jasmine and Keiko went chasing after it, trying to pass the ball to each other the way Sofia had shown them. It wasn't as easy as it looked! Keiko tapped the ball over to Jasmine, but when she tried to bump it back, her foot got tangled up with Keiko's and they both went tumbling to the ground.

Sofia picked up the soccer ball and looked down at her friends, who giggled helplessly. "What happened?" she teased.

Keiko plucked a few blades of grass from her short black hair. "Maybe we took the 'rollover' part too seriously?"

"No such thing as taking soccer too seriously," Sofia joked as she helped Jasmine to her feet.

But before she could help Keiko up, a small, furry sand-colored creature came barreling across the yard and jumped into Keiko's lap, knocking her onto her back again. It was Jasmine's dachshund, Cookie.

"Help!" Keiko cried, shielding her face from the dog, who was licking her affectionately. "He thinks I'm a doggy treat!"

Jasmine quickly pulled Cookie off Keiko. "Sit, Cookie!" she told the dog gently. "Stay! We've worked on this. Manners, remember?"

Cookie sat on his haunches, panting happily as his pink tongue lolled out of the side of his mouth. Ever since the Arroyos had adopted him from the shelter, he'd been the liveliest member of the Arroyo family. So far, Jasmine had taught him how to sit, stay, and shake a paw, but she hadn't quite figured out how to stop the pup from chewing on shoes or jumping on her friends.

Jasmine turned to Keiko, who had scrambled to her feet. "Sorry about that," she told her. "Are you all right?"

Keiko glanced warily at Cookie before giving Jasmine and Sofia a shaky smile. "Yes, I'm fine."

"It's okay if you were scared," Sofia offered. "Cookie *was* pretty ruthless with those doggy kisses."

Hearing his name, Cookie padded over and sat at Keiko's feet. He stared up at her with big brown eyes and rested one paw on her sneaker.

"I think he's apologizing to you," Jasmine explained.

"Oh, it's all right," Keiko said. "He just surprised me."

Jasmine nodded with sympathy. She'd been friends with Keiko long enough to know that she wasn't very comfortable around four-legged creatures. "Dogs still make you nervous, don't they?"

Keiko started to deny it, but there was no use. She sighed and dropped her narrow shoulders. "I'm mostly nervous around bigger dogs like German shepherds. But even the tiny ones scare me sometimes."

Sofia put the soccer ball on the ground and rested her foot on top. "Lots of people are afraid of dogs," she said gently as she swung one of her reddish-brown braids over her shoulder. "You just need more time to get used to them, that's all."

"Can't I just avoid them completely?" Keiko asked.

"You could, but then you'd miss out on the great things about them, too," Jasmine told her friend. In her opinion, dogs were better than ice cream and roller coasters combined. Cookie, for example, was great at playing fetch, and he was always happy to see Jasmine when she got home from school. And he was a champion cuddler, despite his cold, wet nose.

"It's just like the rescued street cats at the shelter," Jasmine continued. She scooped up Cookie as she spoke. "At first, they're super nervous around people, but eventually, they'll eat right out of your hand! Maybe it'll be the same way for you."

"You want Keiko to eat out of your hand?" Sofia asked, giggling.

Jasmine couldn't help smiling. "Ha, ha," she said. "No. I just think the more time she spends with dogs, the less scared she'll be." She turned to Keiko. "You'll see how sweet dogs can be." As if Cookie understood what the girls were talking about, he licked Jasmine's arm lovingly. Jasmine laughed. "See? You're going to love dogs someday."

"You think so?" Keiko asked, sounding unsure.

"Oh, I know so," Jasmine said with complete confidence, grinning at Cookie. "And I know the perfect way for you to start."

A few minutes later, Jasmine had stowed Cookie safely in his crate with a chew toy, and she and her friends sat at the wooden table in Jasmine's kitchen. She told her friends all about how overcrowded Rosa's Refuge was and about Mrs. Wallace's plan to expand. With a serious expression, Jasmine explained what happened to many of the animals that were turned away.

"Wow," Sofia said softly. "I had no idea."

Keiko shook her head sadly. "Me neither."

"What can we do to help?" Sofia asked.

Jasmine quickly explained Mrs. Wallace's plan for the carnival. Then she told her friends some of her ideas about signs and decorations.

"I could use some help assisting Mrs. Wallace," Jasmine explained. "So what do you say?"

"That sounds really cool," Sofia said. "Maybe helping the shelter will prove to my mom and dad how ready I am for a puppy."

Jasmine knew that Sofia had been begging her parents to let her adopt a pet for months, but they weren't convinced that she was ready for the responsibility.

"Are you sure?" asked Keiko with a wince. "Didn't you almost kill the class plant?"

"That was different!" Sofia protested. "I

21

was busy with soccer camp. Plus, plants don't bark to let you know when they need food or water, so really, whose fault is that?"

"Still yours, I think," Keiko said matter-of-factly.

Sofia frowned. "Okay, fine. I'm a plant killer. But I'd be a great dog owner! I know it. I can't wait to pick out a puppy."

"Are you sure you want to start with a puppy?" Jasmine asked. "You have to spend loads of time training them and stuff. What about soccer practice?"

"No sweat!" Sofia said. "The dog can help me practice. If I can keep a ball away from a squirmy little puppy with four legs, the girls on the other team don't stand a chance. And if I help out with the fund-raiser, maybe Mom and

Dad will let me take home one of the rescued dogs."

"Sounds like a good plan to me," Jasmine said. "How about you, Keiko? Can you help?"

Keiko bit her lip and looked away.

"Will I have to be around a lot of dogs?" Keiko asked nervously.

Jasmine shook her head.

"Not if you don't want to be," she said. "The dogs will be at the shelter during the carnival. What I'll really need help with is coming up with lots of creative ideas to make it fun for kids."

Keiko smiled. "In that case, of course I'll help!"

Sofia pulled a piece of paper from Jasmine's notebook and grabbed a pencil. "How about a spin art table?"

"Great idea!" Jasmine cried. "That will be perfect in the arts-and-crafts area. Ooh! And why don't we write little descriptions of each animal that's up for adoption? We can add a photo and put it on a poster that says 'WANTED: A NEW HOME.' Then we can hang the posters all around at the carnival."

"I love it," Sofia agreed, jotting it down. "That's a really cute idea, Jaz."

While they continued to shout out ideas, Keiko remained silent. But finally she leaned forward and said, "I'm not saying I'll get too close, but what if I drew pictures of each of the shelter dogs for the carnival signs? Illustrations might really make the WANTED posters stand out."

"That would be awesome," Jasmine said.

24

She leaned her head back so she could see Cookie's crate. "Did you hear that, Cookie? Keiko's going to help!"

Cookie looked up, barked twice, licked the bars of the crate, and then went back to his toy.

"There you have it," Jasmine told her. "Cookie says, 'Hooray!' Good for you, Keiko. BFFs forever."

Jasmine touched the necklace she always wore and smiled at her friends. It was a simple silver chain with a charm at the end shaped like a dog biscuit. Her name was engraved on the front. Keiko and Sofia had charm necklaces with their names, too. The three friends had picked them out together. Sofia's charm was a soccer ball, and Keiko's was an artist's palette with pretty colored gemstones. As long as the three of them had their special necklaces, Jasmine felt like they would always be friends.

Keiko smirked at Jasmine. "All that with two barks, huh?"

Jasmine shrugged. "What can I say? My dog's a genius."

Chapter 4:
Meeting Madison

That Saturday, Jasmine and her mom drove to the animal shelter as usual. But this time, Jasmine's two best friends were in the backseat with her, talking excitedly about all the ideas they'd come up with for the carnival.

As they pulled into the parking lot, Jasmine saw a hint of worry in Keiko's dark eyes.

"I could just wait in the car, and one of you can take a picture of a dog for me..." Keiko said.

Jasmine shook her head. "No way. You're an artist! You need inspiration! And what could be more inspiring than meeting the animals we're trying to help?"

Keiko groaned. "I guess you're right." But she didn't sound convinced at all.

"Don't worry," Jasmine said. "The Wallaces make sure all the volunteers are safe. Mom and I come here every Saturday, and look"— she held her hands up for inspection—"not a scratch on me."

Keiko looked closer. "There *are* a few scratches."

"Oh, those don't count," Jasmine said, peering at her hands. "They're from the new kittens. They're the cutest. Come on, I'll show you!

You guys can help me finish choosing names for them."

Jasmine climbed out of the car and followed her mom into the animal shelter, with Keiko and Sofia trailing close behind them. She couldn't wait to show her friends around and teach them everything she'd learned as a volunteer.

While her mother went to the room down the hall and to the right, where she treated sick animals, Jasmine gave her friends a tour. She stopped when she reached the doorway that separated the front part of the shelter from the back area, where the kennels were. The door between them was usually kept closed so the barking dogs wouldn't frighten the cats. But the girls could peek into the room through the glass panels in the door. Keiko took one look at the German shepherd who was in the kennel closest to them and backed away nervously.

"I'm not going in there!" Keiko declared.

Jasmine could tell Keiko wasn't kidding. "Okay, we don't have to," she said quickly. "Let's go over here instead."

Jasmine led her friends to a different door. "This is where they keep the younger cats," she said. She twisted the knob and pushed the door open. "And these are my new friends . . ."

Jasmine trailed off when she saw Mrs. Wallace and a girl she didn't recognize crouched on the floor, playing with the kittens.

"Jasmine," Mrs. Wallace said, smiling up at her, "I didn't hear you come in." She got to her feet. "I'd like you to meet our newest volunteer. She lives over in Greenville." She motioned to the girl, who stood up and faced Jasmine and her friends with a big smile. She had wavy red hair pulled back into a messy ponytail and grayish-blue eyes, and wore a bright green dress covered with tiny yellow ducks.

"Hi!" she said brightly. "I'm Madison Rosen."

"Hi, Madison," Jasmine said. "I'm Jasmine, and these are my friends Keiko and Sofia."

"Awesome dress," Keiko said. "I love the colors. Are you an animal expert like Jasmine?"

"I'm no expert, but I know a little," Madison said with a shrug.

"Madison's being modest," Mrs. Wallace said. "She volunteered at the shelter in the town where she lives, and she's been great with the kittens."

Jasmine peered into the box, where the five kittens were busy batting some neon orange plastic balls back and forth. Each time a kitten tapped a ball, it jingled softly.

"It looks like they're playing soccer!" Sofia cried.

"You're right," Madison said. "Their long tails help them balance."

Sofia laughed. "Too bad I can't grow one of those. I'd be the MVP for sure."

"You named this little guy Tiger, right, Jasmine?" Mrs. Wallace said. "Madison came up with names for the rest of the litter."

"I call this one Leo because his fur sticks out like a lion's mane," Madison said, pointing to the golden kitten tumbling in the box, trying to wrestle the plastic ball away from Tiger. "And I call that one Pepper because of his black speckles . . ."

As Mrs. Wallace, Keiko, and Sophie crowded around Madison while she listed the kittens' new names, Jasmine couldn't help feeling a little disappointed. She had been hoping her friends would help her finish naming them today. But Madison seemed nice, and she clearly loved animals as much as Jasmine did. Plus, Jasmine had to admit the names *were* good ones. So Jasmine swallowed her disappointment. She squeezed in next to Madison and stroked Tiger, who began purring loudly.

"He really likes you!" Madison said. She grinned at Jasmine, and Jasmine smiled back.

Chapter 5:
Frisky Frankie

The next Saturday, Mrs. Wallace was waiting for Jasmine and her mom when they arrived for their volunteer shift.

"Good morning!" Mrs. Wallace called brightly. "Dr. Arroyo, you have a patient waiting for you in the exam room."

"I'll head straight there," Jasmine's mother said agreeably as she pulled on her white lab coat. "You know where I'll be if you need me, *niña*," she told Jasmine as she headed toward the exam room.

Mrs. Wallace smiled at Jasmine. "And I have just the job for you!" she said. "Madison arrived about ten minutes ago. She's in the yard walking one of the puppies. Maybe you can lend her a hand."

Mrs. Wallace had surprised Jasmine. She didn't usually let volunteers their age walk the dogs on their own. *She must really trust Madison,* Jasmine thought.

"Okay," Jasmine agreed as she headed outside.

When she stepped into the yard, Madison was trotting around after a large puppy who looked to be part beagle, part terrier, and all trouble! The puppy was on a leash, but he seemed to be leading Madison rather than the other way around.

"Whoa, Frankie!" Madison shouted, her red ponytail swinging. "Slow down!"

"Need help?" Jasmine asked.

"Yes!" Madison said, gasping for breath. "This little guy is running me in circles. He does *not* know how to heel!"

As if in reply, Frankie cocked his head at Jasmine and let out a short, playful bark.

Jasmine planted her hands on her hips. "Okay, I think I know what we need here. I'll be right back."

Jasmine dashed inside and grabbed a small bag from the supply closet. When she got back to the yard, Frankie was still pulling hard on the leash and jumping around Madison excitedly.

"Sit, Frankie!" Madison ordered as she lurched a few feet to the left. Frankie was much stronger than he looked. "Tell me you brought some magic fairy dust that will make him sit still," she pleaded.

"Better," said Jasmine. She held up the bag from the supply closet. "Bacon-flavored dog treats!" She pulled out one and held it in front of Frankie's nose. He immediately stopped bouncing around and stared at the treat as if he were mesmerized.

"Do you want a yummy treat?" Jasmine asked.

Frankie sniffed at it, then licked his snout.

Madison laughed. "I think that means yes."

"If you want it, you're going to have to sit," Jasmine told the pup. She whispered to Madison, "When I say 'sit' and hold my hand out flat, you push his rump down gently."

Madison nodded. "Got it."

"Okay, Frankie," Jasmine said, holding her hand flat above his head. "Sit!"

Madison pushed down on Frankie's behind until he sat.

"Good boy!" Jasmine gushed, and fed him the treat, which he snapped up in seconds. They repeated the routine over and over again until Madison no longer had to touch Frankie's back to get him to sit. All Jasmine had to do was hold her hand flat and say "sit."

"Neat trick," Madison said, impressed.

Jasmine flushed with pride. "Thanks. My

mom showed me how to do it when I got my own puppy."

"So now what?" Madison asked.

"Let's try 'heel,'" Jasmine suggested. "Take the leash and a few treats in your right hand. Now put one treat in your left hand, which should be at your waist. Swing your left hand behind you with the treat in it to get Frankie to circle around so he's right behind your left heel. Once he gets that down, you can try to do it while walking him around the yard."

Madison smiled. "Let's do this."

She and Frankie circled the yard, practicing. As the dog treats disappeared, Frankie became much more obedient. By the end, he was heeling nicely on the first or second try.

"Wow," Madison exclaimed. "This really works!"

Jasmine nodded and smiled encouragingly.

When Frankie's exercise session was over, Madison and Jasmine headed back inside. As Madison led Frankie to his kennel, Jasmine's mom came in.

"Hi, girls," she greeted them. "I'm just taking Sadie for a checkup. Do you two want to help?"

"Sure!" Jasmine said. She loved watching her mom in action.

Jasmine and Madison followed Dr. Arroyo into an exam room. There, she used her stethoscope to listen to the dog's heart. Sadie was a very gentle, older Saint Bernard who had arrived at the shelter just before the Arroyos adopted Cookie. Jasmine loved Sadie's sweet, droopy face, which looked sort of sad in a funny way. She had wanted to take Sadie home, but her parents had pointed out that Sadie was too big for their small house and yard.

Dr. Arroyo peered into Sadie's mouth to make sure her teeth and gums were healthy. Finally, she examined her ears to check for lice and make sure they weren't infected. Jasmine couldn't wait to do the same job someday.

"Is Sadie okay?" Jasmine asked as her mother gently moved Sadie's hind legs up and down and massaged her muscles.

Dr. Arroyo nodded. "Yes, but she does have a touch of arthritis."

"Poor Sadie," Jasmine said. "You can fix it, though, right?"

"Well, there's no cure for arthritis," her mother replied, "but her case isn't too advanced. Some physical therapy and diet supplements should help. And she needs a forever home where she can get a little more exercise. I'll tell Rosa to try to give her an extra walk each day. Would you girls put her back in her kennel?"

"Sure," Jasmine replied, taking Sadie's leash.

"Your friend Keiko is in the after-school art class I just started taking," Madison said. "She's really talented. She texted me a photo of a drawing she made of a dog, and it was so good."

Jasmine felt her shoulders tighten. Keiko and Madison were texting? Jasmine hadn't even known Keiko was in an art class after school. She wondered why Keiko hadn't mentioned it.

At that moment, Mrs. Wallace came by to check on Jasmine and Madison. "How did it go with Frankie?" she asked the girls.

"Great!" Madison said brightly. "Jasmine helped me teach him to sit and heel. She's a real puppy whisperer!"

"I just knew you two would hit it off," Mrs. Wallace said happily. "In fact, I was thinking Madison could help you and your friends with the carnival planning. We need all the help we can get!"

"I'd love to!" Madison gushed eagerly.

"Um, sure," Jasmine agreed, feeling a little deflated. *I thought I was supposed to be Mrs. Wallace's assistant in planning the carnival,* she thought. Still, it would be nice to have more help, and Madison did seem to have a lot of energy. Or was it that Mrs. Wallace thought Madison would have better ideas?

Mrs. Wallace smiled at both girls happily. Suddenly, Jasmine felt foolish for doubting Mrs. Wallace's confidence in her.

"This will be so fun!" Madison exclaimed as she gave Jasmine a huge grin.

"Yes," Jasmine said, returning the smile. "And it will be great for the animals, too!"

If working with Madison would raise more money to expand the shelter, then it was worth it, Jasmine reminded herself. The animals were depending on her!

The next Friday, Jasmine sat down for lunch in the cafeteria across from her best friends. She had told them earlier in the week that Madison would be helping with the carnival, and they were excited.

"I'm sure she'll have great ideas," Sofia said.

"And I've been working on sketches for the WANTED posters," Keiko told them.

"I can't wait to see them," said Jasmine, remembering that Keiko had already texted one of her drawings to Madison. "Hey, why don't you guys come to my house tomorrow morning before my mom drives us to the shelter? We could work on posters and decorations then."

Keiko and Sofia exchanged a look. "Oh, we actually don't need a ride to the shelter tomorrow," Keiko began.

"Oh, okay," Jasmine said, disappointed. Did they not want to come? "But you still want to help out with the carnival, right?" Jasmine asked.

"Of course we do!" Sofia cried, a little too loudly.

Keiko shook her head at Sofia. "See? I told you Jasmine would know something was up." Keiko turned to Jasmine. "I'm terrible at surprises."

"Surprises?" Jasmine asked. What kind of surprise did her friends have for her?

"Keiko's said enough," Sofia said, giggling nervously. "You'll find out tomorrow!"

"Okaaay," Jasmine said with a shrug. She hoped it was something good. It wasn't like her friends to keep things from her.

Keiko patted Jasmine's hand. "Don't worry," she told her friend. "It will be worth the wait. You'll see!"

🐾 🐾 🐾

When Jasmine and her mom got to the shelter the next morning, Jasmine tried to prepare herself before she went in. What were her friends up to? Had they swapped outfits again like they did last April Fools' Day? Or maybe Keiko had drawn a portrait of Cookie as a surprise! There was only one way to find out.

When Jasmine and her mom stepped inside the shelter it was completely empty. There was no Keiko and no Sofia. Even Mrs. Wallace was nowhere to be found.

"Where is everybody?" Jasmine wondered.

Then they heard applause coming from the backyard.

Jasmine and her mom made their way outside. Someone was leading Sadie around the yard. Jasmine blinked. That someone was Keiko!

Her friend Keiko, who usually cringed when she came near even the most adorable puppies, was holding Sadie's leash. Keiko's grip was so tight Jasmine could see her knuckles turning white, but she had a huge, triumphant smile on her face. Sadie looked calm and happy, too.

Jasmine peered past Keiko to see Sofia, Mrs. Wallace, and Madison standing on the far side of the courtyard, clapping and smiling.

With each lap Keiko made, Madison shot her two thumbs up. "Way to go, Keiko!" she called. "You've got this!"

On the third lap, Keiko finally noticed Jasmine standing there. "Jasmine, check it out!" she said. "I'm walking the biggest dog here!"

"Congratulations!" Jasmine cheered, genuinely excited for her friend. But she was confused. When had Keiko decided to do this? Jasmine knew this was a big deal for Keiko.

Why had she told Sofia but not Jasmine what she was planning? Jasmine and her friends always did important things together—especially anything involving animals. And why had Keiko and Sofia kept it a secret? Even Madison had known before Jasmine, she realized, her smile fading.

Keiko handed Sadie's leash to Mrs. Wallace, then ran over and gave Jasmine a warm hug. "Surprise!" Keiko said. "I know how much you wanted me to get over my fear of dogs. So we thought we would surprise you."

"It's—it's wonderful," Jasmine stammered. "I mean, I'm definitely very surprised! How—how did it happen?"

"Well, I told Madison about my fear of dogs during art class," Keiko explained. "Then she told me all about how you had helped her walk Frankie. She mentioned that some of the older dogs are so calm and gentle that they almost walk themselves. Then she encouraged me to try it."

"And it looks like I was right!" Madison said, coming over and giving Keiko a high five.

"Madison met Sofia and me here earlier this week so I could practice," Keiko continued. "I really wanted to impress you!"

"I've been her personal canine cheerleader," Sofia said, grinning.

"Are you really surprised?" Keiko asked, finally noticing the look of confusion on Jasmine's face.

"Definitely!" Jasmine said, forcing a smile. She was happy for Keiko, but she still couldn't help but feel a little like a balloon with all the air let out of it. She'd always thought she'd be the one to help Keiko overcome her fear of dogs. As Jasmine knelt to give Sadie a hug around her big, scruffy neck, though, she realized it didn't matter who got Keiko past her fear. The important thing was that she'd done it.

"Good girl, Sadie," Jasmine said, patting the dog's soft brown-and-white fur. Sadie panted heavily and pushed her big head into Jasmine's chest—her way of asking for more affection. Jasmine smiled. She scratched behind Sadie's ears. Then she stood up and smiled at Keiko. "I couldn't have asked for a more amazing surprise."

The next day, Jasmine's friends were coming over to work on carnival decorations. When Jasmine rushed to answer the doorbell, she was surprised to see Madison standing there next to Sofia and Keiko.

"Hey, Jaz!" Sofia said. "Sorry we're a little late. We stopped to pick up Madison. I thought we could use an extra set of hands." Sofia turned to wave at her mom, who honked twice before pulling off.

Jasmine motioned for them to come in. "Definitely," she said in a friendly voice. "Hi, Madison. How's it going?"

"Great!" Madison cried as she walked past Jasmine and into the house. "I can't wait to get started! This is going to be the best carnival ever."

Jasmine hoped so.

The girls spread out all their art supplies and poster board on the carpeted floor of the living room.

"First we need to make posters to spread the word about the carnival and to advertise the pets who are up for adoption," Jasmine explained. "Then we can decide on decorations."

"I had an idea," Sofia said. "Maybe we can

get lots of different colors of crepe paper and twist it into multicolored streamers to hang from the trees. Since it's a carnival theme, bright colors will work well."

"Oh, that sounds pretty!" Madison said eagerly. "I love rainbows."

"I can start drawing some of my dog sketches on the posters if one of you can do the lettering," Keiko said.

"I'm not great at pictures, but I can do pretty good bubble letters," Sofia offered.

Madison rummaged around in her backpack. "And I brought a bunch of glitter glue pens!" she said, pulling out a handful of sparkly tubes. "These will be great."

"All right!" Keiko exclaimed as she began drawing. Soon, Keiko, Sofia, and Madison were all busily hunched over the poster boards, drawing, lettering, and glittering.

Jasmine wasn't sure what to do. There didn't seem to be space for her around the posters. So she took out a piece of paper and tried brainstorming ideas for other decorations.

"That looks awesome!" Madison said as Keiko handed her a poster with a drawing of a dog under Sofia's bold lettering. "I'll just add some glitter glue, and it will be done!"

"Nice," Sofia said. "Everything is better with sparkles!"

Jasmine twirled her hair as she looked down at her paper, trying to come up with ideas—and trying to shake the feeling that her friends preferred hanging out with Madison to her.

"Hey, what do you all think of balloons

as decorations?" Jasmine asked. "Maybe Mrs. Wallace could get a big balloon arch for the carnival entrance."

Madison looked up from her work, her face serious.

"Balloons are fun, but if some flew off, they might end up in trees or a lake somewhere," she said thoughtfully. "That wouldn't be good for birds, fish, and other animals."

"Oh! Of course!" Jasmine said quickly, her cheeks turning red. She had been so concerned with impressing her friends with her ideas that she had forgotten about the most important thing—the animals!

At that moment, Cookie wandered over to Jasmine and climbed into her lap for a snuggle. He always seemed to know when Jasmine was feeling down and needed some cheering up. Nothing made Jaz feel better than a good puppy cuddle.

"Your dog is the cutest," Madison said. Then she scooted over and gestured to Jasmine to join her. "I could use some help with this glitter. Which color do you want to use?"

"Red would work," Jasmine said, giving Madison a grateful smile. Then she picked up Cookie and placed him next to her so she had some room to work. She felt better already.

That night after dinner, instead of hanging around for dessert, Jasmine went to her room. She gazed at the bulletin board filled with photographs of her, Sofia, and Keiko. She smiled at the photo from Halloween, when they had all dressed up like cats, with fake whiskers sprouting from under their noses.

They'd always been so close. But lately, things seemed different, and Jasmine had to admit it bothered her. To take her mind off her friends, she decided to make some more carnival decorations on her own. When she concentrated on the needy animals at the shelter, her worries seemed smaller.

"Hi, honey," her mom said, popping her head into Jasmine's room. "How's it going in here? All set for the carnival next weekend?"

Jasmine shrugged. "Yeah, I guess," she said.

Her mom stepped into the room, taking a seat on Jasmine's bed, which was covered with a baby-blue comforter, Jasmine's favorite color.

"Is everything okay, *niña*?" she asked. "You hardly said a word during dinner, and you haven't said good night to Cookie."

Jasmine could never hide anything from her mom. Ever since she was little, her mom could always tell what kind of mood she was in. "Can I tell you something?" Jasmine asked her mom now.

"Of course," Dr. Arroyo said. "You can tell me anything."

Jasmine stared at the floor. "I . . . I think Sofia and Keiko like Madison more than me."

"What makes you say that?" her mom asked. "I thought you were all friends."

Jasmine nodded. "We are. That's why I haven't said anything." She looked down, embarrassed.

"You know, friends don't have to do everything together," her mom pointed out.

Jasmine looked up at her mom in surprise. "They don't?"

She laughed softly. "No. I realize you, Sofia, and Keiko are used to doing almost everything together. But sometimes it's okay to give people a little space. They're still your friends."

"Are you sure?" Jasmine asked.

Her mom squeezed her hand. "I'm positive. If they weren't, they wouldn't be working so hard on this carnival for the shelter. That's more your cause than theirs, and they wouldn't be helping if they didn't care about you."

Jasmine studied her mom's light brown eyes. "Maybe you're right," she said. Jasmine was too tired to talk about it anymore. She gave her mom a hug as she stifled a yawn. "Thanks, Mom."

Jasmine turned off her desk lamp and climbed under the covers. "Oh! I forgot one last thing. Here, Cookie!"

A minute later, the dog appeared at the door. Jasmine's mom picked him up and laid him on the bed. Cookie yipped, turned in a long circle, and burrowed under the covers next to Jasmine.

Jasmine smiled. *Dogs are the best*, she thought. Cuddling with Cookie always made her feel safe and warm. This thought reminded her that there were a lot of stray dogs out there who needed homes of their own, or at least a safe place at Rosa's Refuge until a permanent home could be found. And it was up to Jasmine and her friends to help them.

Chapter 8:
A Major Mistake

The weather could not have been more beautiful on the day of the carnival. Jasmine and her parents, along with many of the other regular shelter volunteers, arrived early to help set up. Jasmine's dad helped her hang the WANTED posters all around the park. Then they draped the colorful crepe paper streamers from tree branches. Everything looked very festive.

Mrs. Wallace buzzed around, a clipboard in hand.

"Hi, Jasmine!" she called out as she hurried by. "You and your family are doing a great job with the decorations. And tell your mom I said thanks so much for taking care of the food!"

The food? Jasmine thought. *What food?* Just then, her mom greeted someone behind Jasmine.

Jasmine spun around. "Tía Alicia?" she said in surprise. "What are you doing here?"

"Your mother told me how much you are doing to help the animal shelter, and I wanted to help out, too," her aunt said as she wrapped Jasmine in a big hug. "So I agreed to donate food for the carnival."

She gestured to the table behind her, where servers from El Coquí Café, her aunt's Caribbean restaurant, were busy unloading a van. They set up aluminum trays filled with empanadas, yellow rice, and roasted meats. There were also pitchers of lemonade and iced tea and trays of fresh fruit.

"Wow!" Jasmine said. "Thank you, Tía Alicia!"

Her mouth watered at the sight of all that delicious traditional Puerto Rican food. There were even two trays of Jasmine's favorite dish— sweet plantains. She'd watched many times as her aunt cut off the hard peel of the plantains, which looked like long bananas, and sliced the plantains into small flat pieces, then fried them until they were golden brown.

"I have to get back to the café," her aunt said as she kissed Jasmine. "But I wanted to be sure it all got here on time."

"I just saw Madison, Sofia, and Keiko in the

arts-and-crafts corner," said Jasmine's mother. "Why don't you go see if your friends could use some help?"

"Okay, see you later!" Jasmine said. As she walked across the park, she noted the bounce castle and petting zoo in one corner. There were fluffy ducklings, two sheep, a goat, and even a small pony giving children rides in a little loop! Then there was a donation tent, where people could buy T-shirts, make a donation, or enter the raffle. There was a games tent and even a small stage, where a local band was setting up their instruments. The carnival looked even more wonderful than Jasmine had imagined!

As Jasmine approached the arts-and-crafts corner, she saw an adult volunteer running the spin art station, which already had a line of five or six kids waiting to make a painting. Nearby, several picnic tables were set up with cups of crayons, colored pencils, and stacks of paper. Keiko, Sofia, and Madison were huddled together there, whispering.

"Hey, guys!" Jasmine called with a wave.

But when the girls saw her, instead of waving back, they quickly broke their huddle. Madison snatched the paper they'd been looking at and hid it behind her back. Then they turned and faced Jasmine, shoulder to shoulder.

"Oh, hi," Sofia said, shifting her eyes to Keiko, who glanced at Madison.

Sensing that something was off, Jasmine shuffled her feet uncertainly. "Um, what's going on?"

Keiko blinked innocently. "What do you mean? Nothing's going on."

"Don't you love how Mrs. Wallace turned our arts-and-crafts corner into an art gallery?" Madison asked, changing the subject.

"An art gallery?" Jasmine asked.

Keiko stepped back and pointed at a bunch of drawings of some of the shelter animals that were now hanging from colored yarn strung between two trees.

"Jasmine?" Keiko asked, puzzled. "Don't you like the art gallery?"

"Oh! It's great," Jasmine said, focusing on the drawings, which were clipped up with cute plastic clothespins. She recognized a picture of Frankie and one of the five kittens, drawn in crooked orange crayon.

"After kids come here to draw pictures of the animals," Keiko said, "we post them on this board for people to buy. All the money goes to the shelter. Isn't that awesome?"

Jasmine nodded. She loved the art gallery, but it still felt like her friends were hiding something. "What's that in your hand?" Jasmine asked Madison. "Is it another picture?"

Madison's eyes went wide. "It's nothing. Just something I have to give my mom." She glanced off in the distance. "I think I hear her calling me now! I'll be right back." With that, she took off like a shot. As she ran, Sofia and Keiko struggled to hold in their giggles.

Jasmine's stomach twisted. Were they laughing at her? "What's so funny?" she demanded. "What are you leaving me out of now?"

Keiko wrinkled her nose in confusion. "What do you mean? When did we leave you out?"

"Well, you didn't include me when you decided to try walking Sadie at the shelter," Jasmine said sadly. "And you never told me Madison was in your art class. And now the three of you are laughing at me!"

Sofia shook her head. "We're not laughing at you. Madison just—"

"I don't want to hear any more about Madison!" Jasmine cried. "I wish it was just us again."

Suddenly, Keiko glanced past Jasmine, and her eyes widened. When Jasmine turned to follow her gaze, she found Madison standing right behind her. She'd returned just in time to hear

Jasmine. Without saying a word, Madison bowed her head, turned around, and quickly walked away. Jasmine didn't need to see Madison's eyes to know they were probably full of tears.

Jasmine felt awful. Even worse, when she turned back to her friends, she saw the same hurt expressions on their faces. Jasmine stood there for a moment, not sure what to say. Finally, she turned and walked away. She knew she had messed up. She had just been honest, but she hadn't meant for Madison to hear. Was everyone mad at her now?

Chapter 9:
A New Forever Friend

Jasmine found a quiet bench to sit on. She ran her finger over her dog-biscuit-shaped necklace. What a day this was turning out to be!

"Can I sit with you?" someone asked.

Jasmine glanced up to see Keiko.

"Of course you can!" Jasmine said. She scooted over to make room.

"Is there space for me, too?" another voice chimed in. Jasmine smiled as she slid over to make a spot for Sofia as well.

Keiko handed Jasmine a brown manila envelope with *Jasmine* written in swirly glitter ink.

"We were saving this for the end of the carnival, but I think you should open it now," Keiko said. She handed it to Jasmine.

Jasmine opened the envelope to find a giant homemade card. On the front was a drawing of Jasmine holding Cookie and smiling. It looked like something Keiko had drawn. She opened the card and gasped. Every inch was covered in ink. All the shelter volunteers had signed it. They'd left little notes thanking her for her hard work.

"Sofia, Madison, and I wanted to thank you for getting us involved with the shelter and the carnival," Keiko explained. "So we got everyone to sign the card—and make a donation to the shelter in your name."

Jasmine was stunned. "Wow! This is the nicest thing anyone has ever done for me. Thank you both so much!"

"You're welcome," Sofia said. "But really, you should thank Madison. It was her idea."

"Madison's idea?" Jasmine asked.

"Maybe you should read what she wrote," Keiko suggested, pointing to a scribbled message near the bottom left corner.

Dear Jasmine,

Thank you for helping me with Frankie and for being my friend. It means a lot to me. And thank you for sharing your friends Keiko and Sofia!

Love,

Madison

"We were finishing the card up when you surprised us at the art station. I'm sorry you thought we were doing something fun without you," Sofia said. "We wanted to keep it a secret so we could give it to you as a present."

"I'm sorry, too!" Jasmine cried. She threw her arms around Sofia. Then she turned to hug Keiko. "I feel really bad for what I said about Madison. I have to go find her and apologize." She jumped up from the bench. "Will you both go with me?" she asked.

"Of course," Keiko replied.

"That's what friends are for!" Sofia added.

Keiko, Jasmine, and Sofia walked across the park, looking for Madison. After a few minutes, they found her outside the adopt-a-cat trailer.

She was checking up on the five stray kittens, who were curled up in a cage with one of Jasmine's WANTED: A NEW HOME posters next to it.

"Hi, Madison," Jasmine said. "I wanted to thank you for this." She held up her card. "This is one of the nicest things anyone's ever done for me, and Keiko said it was your idea!"

Madison straightened up and smiled shyly. "You're welcome," she said. "I wanted to do something for you, since you've done so much for the shelter—and for me."

"For you?" Jasmine asked, surprised. "I don't feel like I did anything nice for you. I'm really sorry about what I said. I didn't mean it. I just thought you, Sofia, and Keiko were having more fun without me around."

"I'm sorry, too!" Madison exclaimed. "I

didn't mean for our surprise to make you feel left out. I was just so happy to meet all of you at the shelter and find friends who liked animals as much as me. No one at my school is like that." Madison's shoulders drooped.

"Really?" Sofia asked.

"Yeah," Madison said. "I'm known at school for being, well, a little *too* into animals."

"What do you mean?" Jasmine asked, puzzled. She didn't think it was possible to love animals too much!

"Well, my school used to have some classroom pets—mostly mice and hamsters—in cages," Madison explained. "They were meant for us to learn about animals, but to me they looked sad locked up like that. So one day when the teacher wasn't looking, I set them free."

Jasmine's eyes bulged. "You didn't!"

"I did," Madison said.

"But what if the animals couldn't take care of themselves on their own?" Jasmine asked.

"I didn't think about that at the time," Madison replied. "I know now that it was a big mistake, but then, well . . . I thought I was helping them."

Jasmine knew how Madison felt. She had made a similar mistake when she suggested a balloon arch as a carnival decoration. It was important to think things through, especially where animals were concerned.

"Anyway, my mom decided I needed a place to go to show my love for animals in a better way," Madison continued. "We're moving here next month, and my mom thought I might also meet some friends in our new neighborhood. I'm finishing the year at my old school, but next fall, I'll be at the same school as you, Keiko, and Sofia."

"Really?" Keiko said. "That's great news!"

"I didn't think so at first," Madison admitted. "I was scared to move here and be the new girl starting at a different school. It's hard not knowing anyone."

Jasmine tried to picture what that would be like. She'd always lived in the same place with the same people, and she'd known her best friends for years. It would be scary to start over somewhere new.

"That's why when I met all of you I tried really hard to become instant best friends—maybe too hard," Madison explained. "I just liked you all so much."

"But we like you, too!" Jasmine insisted. "Friends?" She held out her pinkie.

Madison hooked her pinkie around Jasmine's. "Friends," she agreed. The girls grinned.

Sofia cleared her throat. "I hate to break up this touching moment, but can we please check in on some animals soon? My parents are here, but they haven't seen me with any dogs or even cats. At this rate, I'll never get a dog!"

Chapter 10:
Terrific Teamwork

The four girls were about to step inside the adopt-a-cat trailer to see if they could help there when Mrs. Wallace flagged them down.

"Girls!" she said breathlessly. "There's a long line at the petting zoo. Do you think you could head over there to help?"

"We're on it!" Jasmine said eagerly as she and her friends changed course. The animal handlers who had set up the petting zoo waved the girls past the line of families waiting to get inside the roped-off area that held the ducks, sheep, and goats.

"What can we do?" Madison asked one of the handlers.

"Just make sure everyone's happy while they're waiting in line and that they head outside of the ropes once they've had their turn," he said.

Together, the four girls worked as a team. Madison helped keep the line moving by handing out paper cups of food pellets to the kids who wanted to feed the goats and sheep, while Keiko snapped pictures of the kids petting the ducklings. Since Jasmine knew the most about animals, she told the kids a little bit about each one and ushered them out when they were done. Meanwhile, Sofia helped the younger children climb on and off the Shetland pony before and after their rides. She even cleaned up after the pony and held the lead rope while the pony handler lifted kids on and off. Jasmine saw Sofia's parents watching her from afar. They looked impressed.

Soon the line at the petting zoo was much shorter, and the girls were free to go.

They were heading back to the adopt-a-cat trailer when Mr. Wallace stepped up to the microphone on the stage.

"Would everyone please gather around?" he announced. "It's time for the raffle!"

The girls headed toward the stage, where they joined up with Jasmine's dad and Sofia's parents. Mrs. Wallace and Jasmine's mother were standing on the stage behind the microphone, holding a large glass bowl full of tiny red tickets. When Mrs. Wallace noticed the girls walk up, she tapped the microphone.

She cleared her throat. "Please get out your raffle tickets!" she said.

People in the crowd reached into their pockets or wallets and pulled out the red ticket stubs they had bought to enter the raffle. Dr. Arroyo held the bowl while Mrs. Wallace reached inside and drew out a ticket.

"Number one-three-five-eight!" she called into the microphone.

A girl near the front screamed, "That's me!" and climbed onto the stage, where she received movie tickets and a tub of popcorn. Mrs. Wallace called another number and someone won tickets to a baseball game.

When Mrs. Wallace called the final number, the winner was someone Jasmine knew—Sofia's mom!

Sofia's mom looked a bit sheepish as she accepted the prize from a local pet store—a dog bed, a water and food dish, a shiny dog collar, a bag of food, and a brush.

"We don't even have a dog," she whispered to Mrs. Wallace as she stepped off the stage.

"It's a sign!" Jasmine shouted.

"It's a coincidence," Keiko countered dryly.

"It's perfect," Sofia said, rubbing her hands together happily. "One more reason for them to get me a dog someday."

Once all the fanfare from the raffle died down, Mrs. Wallace continued. "I want to thank you all so much for coming today to support Rosa's Refuge!"

Everyone clapped politely.

"Thanks to this wonderful community, we have raised the money we need to expand the shelter!"

This time the crowd whooped and cheered, especially Jasmine and her friends.

"We couldn't have pulled this off without every one of you pitching in," Mrs. Wallace said. "I'd like to thank my friend Justin Wheeler for providing the animals in the petting zoo, and El Coquí Café for donating the delicious food. And of course I'd like to thank all my volunteers. But right now I'd like to thank four of our most dedicated volunteers. They had the idea to make the fantastic posters you've seen around the park featuring our shelter animals in need of homes. Thanks to Keiko Hayashi, Sofia Davis, Madison Rosen, and Jasmine Arroyo, we may have found many of our furry friends forever homes! Come on up here, girls, and take a bow."

Jasmine and her friends made their way to the stage. The entire crowd was clapping and cheering for them. It felt amazing. But knowing that they'd helped the animals felt even better.

The next weekend, Jasmine, Sofia, Keiko, and Madison were at the shelter bright and early Saturday morning.

At the end of their shift, Jasmine had a surprise for Madison.

"Sofia, Keiko, and I wanted to get you a real welcome present so you'll always feel at home here in your new town," Jasmine explained.

She handed Madison a small box wrapped in glossy paper decorated with cats.

"Open it! Open it!" Keiko cried, barely able to contain her excitement.

Madison tore away the paper and opened the box. Inside was a simple silver chain with a kitten charm engraved with her name. It was the same type of charm as the ones Jasmine, Sofia, and Keiko had.

Madison squealed. "I love it!"

"Good," Jasmine said with a smile. "Because we're all best friends *fur*ever now."

"Yeah, good luck getting rid of us," Sofia added.

As Jasmine watched Madison slip her new necklace over her head, she felt like the luckiest girl in town. Not only had she helped the animal shelter, but she had found a new friend as well—one who loved animals as much as she did.

Don't miss the next **forever friends** book!

Madison's New Buddy

Madison loves volunteering at the animal shelter with her new friends Jasmine, Keiko, and Sofia. And when Jasmine comes up with the idea of a school project to read to the dogs to help them relax, Madison wants to help. But she's worried that her friends—and her classmates—will discover that she's not a strong reader.

Then Madison is paired with Buddy, a nervous golden retriever puppy who's new to the shelter. If Buddy doesn't get over his fear of people, he might not get adopted! If reading aloud to him helps, Madison's willing to try, even if it means letting her friends in on her secret.

A group of girls so close, they're just

Like Sisters

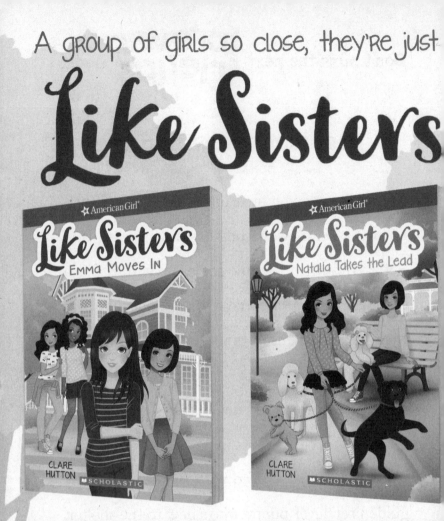

Emma loves visiting her twin cousins, Natalia and Zoe, so she's thrilled when her family moves to their town after living 3,000 miles away. Emma knows her life is about to change in a big way. And it will be more wonderful and challenging than any of the girls expect!

Several dogs are staying with their owners at the family's B&B. Natalia eagerly volunteers to watch a walk all of them with the help of her sister Zoe an her cousin Emma. But Zoe and Emma have their ow commitments, and Natalia is quickly overwhelme When one of the dogs goes missing, will Natalia b able to step up and make things right?